KATIE MORAG and the TWO GRANDMOTHERS

High Farm

The Holiday House

Mrs Bayview's

The Lady Art

The Redburn Bridge

The Village

THE ISLE of STRUAY

Grannie's

The Mainland

The Jetty

ISLE of STRUAY
SHOP & POST OFFICE

OBAN TIMES
GET YOUR COPY HERE

The Shop & Post Office

ALSO BY MAIRI HEDDERWICK IN RED FOX

Katie Morag and the New Pier
Katie Morag Delivers the Mail
Katie Morag and the Wedding
Oh No, Peedie Peebles!

A Red Fox Book

Published by Random House Children's Books
20 Vauxhall Bridge Road, London SW1V 2SA

A division of Random House UK Ltd
London Melbourne Sydney Auckland
Johannesburg and agencies throughout the world

Copyright © Mairi Hedderwick 1985

1 3 5 7 9 10 8 6 4 2

First published in Great Britain
by The Bodley Head Children's Books 1985
Red Fox edition 1997

Printed in China

RANDOM HOUSE UK Limited Reg. No. 954009

ISBN 0 09 911871 8

To all Grandmothers – Big or Wee

KATIE MORAG and the TWO GRANDMOTHERS

Mairi Hedderwick

RED FOX

One sunny Wednesday morning Mrs McColl woke Katie Morag early.

"Hurry up, now!" she said, drawing back the curtains. "Here comes the boat. Granma Mainland will be here soon and you've still got this room to tidy for her."

Granma Mainland lived far away in the big city. She was coming to stay with them for a holiday.

Katie Morag went with her other grandmother, Grannie Island, who lived just across the Bay, to meet the boat.

"My, you're still a smart wee Bobby Dazzler," said Neilly Beag, as he helped Granma Mainland down.

Grannie Island revved the engine *very* loudly. BUROOM . . . BUROOM . . . BUROOM . . .

Katie Morag watched, fascinated, as Granma Mainland unpacked.

"Do you like this new hat I've brought for Show Day, Katie Morag?" Granma Mainland asked.

"Och, her and her fancy ways!" muttered Grannie Island to herself.

Show Day was always a big event on the Island of Struay. At the Post Office, Mr and Mrs McColl were rushed off their feet.

"*Look* where you're GOING!" shouted Mrs McColl, as Katie Morag tripped over baby Liam.

"Katie Morag, I think you'd be better off helping Grannie Island get Alecina ready for the Show," sighed Mr McColl.

Alecina was Grannie Island's prize sheep. She had won the Best Ewe and
Fleece Trophy for the past seven years, but she was getting old, and everyone
said that Neilly Beag's April Love would win it this year.

HOME
PRODUCE

HANDICRAFTS

Pets'
Corner

Katie Morag ran as fast as she could, past the Show Field, where frantic last-minute preparations were in progress, and on to Grannie Island's in order to give Alecina an extra special brush and comb before the judging started.

Refreshments

BAYVIEW BARROW

But when Katie Morag arrived at Grannie Island's, Alecina was up to her horns in the Boggy Loch.

"A whole hillside to eat and she wants *that* blade of grass!" cried Grannie Island in a fury.

"Look at your fleece! And today of *all* days, you old devil!" ranted Grannie Island when they eventually got Alecina out of the Boggy Loch. "We'll never get these peaty stains out in time for the Show!"

"Granma Mainland has some stuff to make *her* hair silvery white . . ." said Katie Morag thoughtfully.

Everyone looked in amazement as Grannie Island's old tractor and trailer hurtled past the Show Field, heading for the Post Office.
"We'll be too late!" grumbled Grannie Island.

Fortunately, no one was about when they got home, since Mrs McColl
would certainly not have approved of this . . .

. . . or this.

And Granma Mainland would have been furious at this . . .

. . . not to mention this.

But all ended well. They managed to get tidied up and back to the Show Field just in time for the judging, and, at the sight of Alecina's shiny coat and curls, the judges were in no doubt as to who should win the Silver Trophy again this year.

That evening there was a party at Grannie Island's to celebrate.

"My, but thon old ewe is still some beauty for her age," said Neilly Beag.

"Just like yourself, Granma Mainland. How do you do it?"

"Ah, that's *my* secret," said wee Granma Mainland, fluttering her eyelashes.

Katie Morag and Grannie Island smiled at each other. They knew some of the secret, but would never tell.

And Grannie Island never frowned at Granma Mainland's "fancy ways" ever again. I wonder why?

Some bestselling Red Fox picture books

THE BIG ALFIE AND ANNIE ROSE STORYBOOK
by Shirley Hughes
OLD BEAR
by Jane Hissey
OI! GET OFF OUR TRAIN
by John Burningham
DON'T DO THAT!
by Tony Ross
NOT NOW, BERNARD
by David McKee
ALL JOIN IN
by Quentin Blake
THE WHALES' SONG
by Gary Blythe and Dyan Sheldon
JESUS' CHRISTMAS PARTY
by Nicholas Allan
THE PATCHWORK CAT
by Nicola Bayley and William Mayne
MATILDA
by Hilaire Belloc and Posy Simmonds
WILLY AND HUGH
by Anthony Browne
THE WINTER HEDGEHOG
by Ann and Reg Cartwright
A DARK, DARK TALE
by Ruth Brown
HARRY, THE DIRTY DOG
by Gene Zion and Margaret Bloy Graham
DR XARGLE'S BOOK OF EARTHLETS
by Jeanne Willis and Tony Ross
WHERE'S THE BABY?
by Pat Hutchins